Franklin's Bad Day

ISBN 0-590-69332-8

Text copyright © 1997 by Paulette Bourgeois
Illustrations copyright © 1997 by Brenda Clark
FRANKLIN and the FRANKLIN character are trademarks of
Kids Can Press Ltd.
All rights reserved. Published by Scholastic Inc., 555 Broadway, New York,
NY 10012, by arrangement with Kids Can Press Ltd.
Interior illustrations prepared with the assistance of Muriel Hughes Wood.

12 11 10 9 8 7 6 5 4 3 2 1   7 8 9/9 0 1 2/0

Printed in the U.S.A.   09

First Scholastic printing, January 1997

Franklin's Bad Day

Paulette Bourgeois
Brenda Clark

SCHOLASTIC INC.
New York   Toronto   London   Auckland   Sydney

FRANKLIN loved to play outside in winter. He could skate forward and backward. He liked to catch snowflakes on his tongue and make angels in the snow. But today was different. Franklin was having a very bad day.

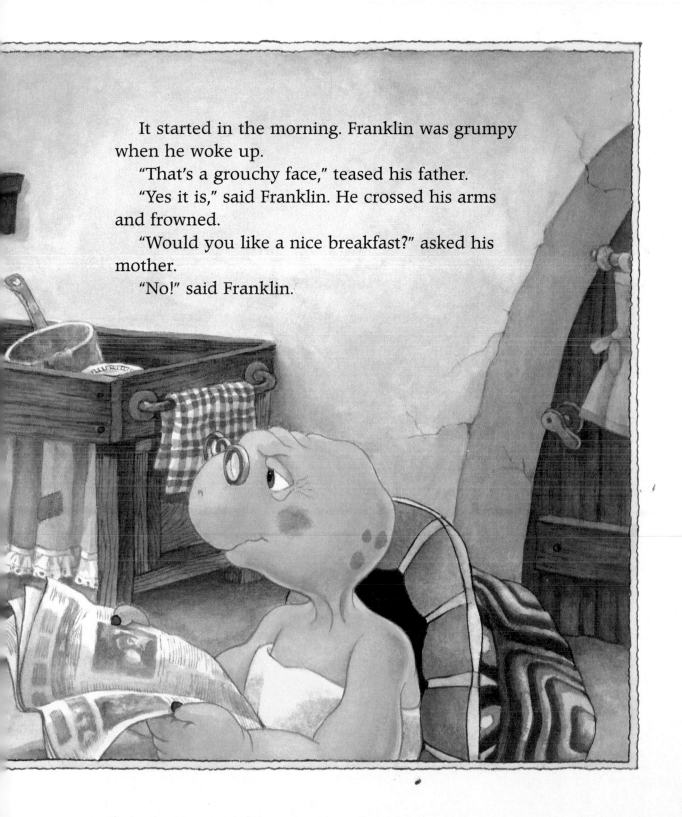

It started in the morning. Franklin was grumpy when he woke up.

"That's a grouchy face," teased his father.

"Yes it is," said Franklin. He crossed his arms and frowned.

"Would you like a nice breakfast?" asked his mother.

"No!" said Franklin.

His mother made breakfast anyway.

Franklin stared out the window. Heavy gray clouds pushed across the sky.

"It's even a bad day outside," grumbled Franklin. He picked at his food.

For the rest of the morning, nothing went right.
Franklin knocked over his juice and broke his
favorite cup. He couldn't find his marbles, and the
last piece of his puzzle was missing.
Franklin slammed a door and stomped his feet.
"You seem awfully cranky," said his mother.
"I am not!" shouted Franklin.

Just then, Bear knocked on the door. Franklin peeked out.

"Do you want to make a snowman or ride on my sled?" asked Bear.

Franklin sighed. "I don't want to do *anything*."

"Please?" Bear said.

"Fresh air will do you good," said his parents. "Out you go with Bear."

They handed Franklin his hat and mittens.

Franklin pouted as he bundled up and went outside.

The two friends walked along the path near
Otter's house.

"Let's ask Otter to come," said Bear.

Franklin gave Bear a puzzled look.

"Oh, I forgot," said Bear sadly. "Otter moved
away yesterday."

They didn't talk all the way to the hill.

Franklin kneeled at the front of the sled and
Bear sat behind him.

Bear gave a push. "Let's go!" he shouted.

The sled glided halfway down the slope. And
then it stopped. They had landed on a bare patch.

"Oh no!" wailed Franklin. "What a terrible day!"

The hill was no fun, so Beaver suggested they go to the pond.

When they arrived, the pond was roped off.

"No skating today," warned Mr. Mole. "The ice is thin."

Franklin lost his temper. "This is my worstest day ever!"

"There's no such word as worstest," said Beaver.

"There is for me!" said Franklin. "I'm leaving!"

Franklin stormed home.

He threw his skates and his slushy, mushy mittens on the floor.

"Please pick up your things," said his mother.

"NO!" he yelled.

Franklin was sent to his room.

Franklin was so furious that he kicked
his castle.

His father came running when he heard the
crash. "What's going on in here?"

Franklin lay on the floor and cried.

"Don't worry," said his father. "You can build
the castle again."

"But I made that castle with Otter, and she's
not here anymore," sobbed Franklin.

"Oh, now I understand," said Franklin's father. "You're mad and sad because your friend moved away."

Franklin nodded.

"And you miss her a lot," his father said.

"Yes," agreed Franklin in a small voice.

They hugged each other for a long time.

"Otter and I did lots of things together," said Franklin. "Now we can't."

"You can still be friends," said Franklin's father. "You can share your feelings by calling or writing."

Franklin thought for a moment.

"Do we have a big envelope and some stamps?" he asked.

Franklin spent the rest of the day making
a scrapbook for Otter.

He filled it with pictures and drawings of the
two friends together.

Near the back, Franklin put a dozen
envelopes. He printed his address on each one.

On the last page, he wrote:

> *Please write to me. Then we can*
> *stay friends forever.*

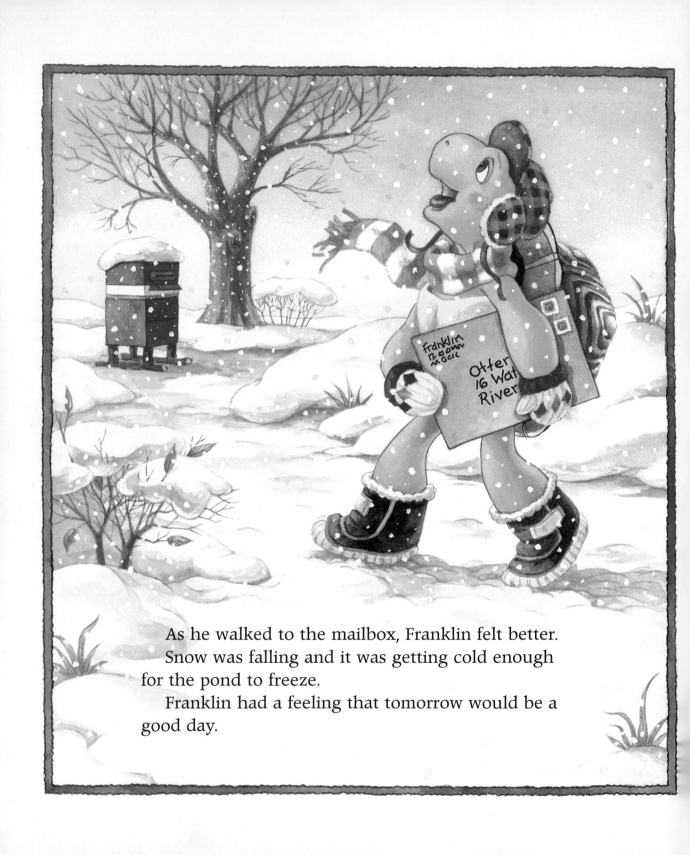

As he walked to the mailbox, Franklin felt better. Snow was falling and it was getting cold enough for the pond to freeze.

Franklin had a feeling that tomorrow would be a good day.